Disney

FROZEN

Storybook Collection

Disney PRESS

Los Angeles · New York

CONTENTS

Printed in the United States of America

First Edition, September 2016

2 4 6 8 10 9 7 5 3 1

FAC-038091-16225

Library of Congress Control Number: 2015946850

ISBN 978-1-4847-5873-1

For more Disney Press fun, visit www.disneybooks.com

SUSTAINABLE FORESTRY INITIATIVE Certified Sourcing
www.sfiprogram.org
SFI-00993
This Label Applies to Text Stock Only

THE KINGDOM OF ARENDELLE was a happy place. The king and queen had two young daughters, Anna and Elsa. But the family had a secret: Elsa could create ice and snow with her hands. One night, Anna convinced Elsa to turn the ballroom into a winter wonderland. As the sisters happily played together, Elsa accidentally lost control of her magic. An icy blast hit Anna in the head, and she fell to the floor, unconscious.

The king and queen rushed the girls to the trolls, mysterious healers who knew about magic. A wise troll named Grand Pabbie saved Anna by removing her memories of Elsa's magic. He explained that she was lucky to have been hit in the head, not in the heart.

The troll told the king and queen that Elsa's powers would only grow stronger. "Fear will be her enemy," he warned.

The king and queen knew they had to protect their daughter. To keep her magic a secret, they closed the kingdom's gates. The king gave Elsa gloves to contain her powers, but she was still afraid she might hurt someone. She even avoided Anna to keep her safe. Then, when Anna and Elsa were teenagers, their parents were lost at sea. The sisters had never felt more alone.

Elsa stayed inside, where she could hide her magic. But she could not keep the castle gates closed forever. On the day of her coronation, her subjects were invited inside to celebrate.

Elsa was nervous, but Anna was thrilled at the chance to meet new people! She had barely stepped outside the castle when she met Prince Hans of the Southern Isles. Anna was smitten with the handsome prince. The two instantly fell in love.

At the coronation ball, Prince Hans asked Anna to marry him. Anna said yes right away, and the couple went to ask Elsa for her blessing.

Elsa refused to bless the marriage. She couldn't let her younger sister marry a man she had just met!

Anna couldn't believe Elsa. "Why do you shut me out? What are you so afraid of?" she cried angrily.

As Elsa fought with her sister, she lost control of her magic. Ice shot from her hands. Now all of Arendelle knew her secret. Panicked, Elsa fled into the mountains.

With her secret out, Elsa let her powers loose. A storm raged around her as she created an ice palace and even changed the way she looked. Below her, ice and snow covered Arendelle.

Anna felt awful! Leaving Hans in charge, she went after her sister.

As Anna trekked through the forest, she lost her horse. Luckily, she met an ice harvester named Kristoff and his reindeer, Sven. The two agreed to help her find Elsa.

High in the mountains, Anna and Kristoff came across a dazzling winter wonderland, where they met a living snowman.

"I'm Olaf," the snowman said.

Anna realized that Elsa must have created him. She asked Olaf to lead them to Elsa so she could bring back summer. Olaf loved the idea of summer and happily led them to Elsa's palace.

Inside, Anna told Elsa about Arendelle's winter storm.

"It's okay. You can just unfreeze it," she said.

But Elsa didn't know how to stop the snow and the winter storm. Frustrated, she cried out, "I can't!"

An icy blast shot across the room and hit Anna in the heart!

Kristoff rushed forward to help Anna. "I think we should go," he said.

At the base of the mountain, Kristoff noticed that Anna's hair was beginning to turn white. He knew his friends the trolls would be able to help her.

Grand Pabbie saw at once that Anna was hurt. "There is ice in your heart, put there by your sister," he said gravely. "If not removed, to solid ice you will freeze, forever."

Grand Pabbie explained that only an act of true love could thaw a frozen heart. Anna knew Hans was her true love. Maybe a kiss from him would save her heart from freezing!

Anna, Kristoff, Sven, and Olaf raced back to Arendelle to find Prince Hans.

But Hans was not in Arendelle. He had set out to look for Anna when her horse returned without her.

Hans and the search party arrived at Elsa's palace. The men attacked Elsa, and she defended herself. One of the men aimed a crossbow at Elsa! Hans pushed it aside, and the arrow hit a chandelier. It crashed to the ground, knocking Elsa out.

Hans and his men took the queen back to Arendelle and threw her in the castle's dungeon.

Outside the kingdom, Anna, Kristoff, Olaf, and Sven hurried down the mountain. Anna was getting weaker by the minute. Kristoff was worried about her. At the castle gates, he passed her to the royal servants. He was starting to realize that he cared

deeply about Anna, but he knew her true love, Hans, could make her well again.

Anna found Hans in the library. She asked him to save her life with a kiss, but he refused! Hans had only been pretending to love Anna so he could take over Arendelle. He put out the room's fire and left Anna to freeze.

In the dungeon, all Elsa could think about was getting away from Arendelle. It was the only way to protect everyone, especially Anna, from her powers. Elsa became so upset that she froze the whole dungeon and escaped!

Alone in the library, Anna realized how reckless she had been. In trying to find love, she had doomed her sister and herself.

Just when Anna had given up all hope, Olaf burst through the door. The snowman lit a fire to warm her.

Anna worried that the fire would melt Olaf, but the snowman didn't care. "Some people are worth melting for," he said.

Just then, Olaf looked out the window. He saw Kristoff riding back toward the castle on Sven. The snowman realized that Kristoff was Anna's true love!

Olaf helped Anna outside. Then she saw Hans about to strike Elsa with his sword! Anna threw herself in front of Elsa. Hans's sword came down just as Anna's body froze to solid ice.

Elsa wrapped her arms around her frozen sister. "Oh, Anna," she sobbed. Then something amazing happened: Anna began to thaw!

"An act of true love will thaw a frozen heart," Olaf said.

"Love!" Elsa cried, looking at Anna. "That's it!" Love was the key to her magic. She reversed the winter and brought back summer.

With summer restored, Arendelle returned to normal—but from then on, the castle gates were open for good. For the first time in a long while, Arendelle was a happy place again. And Queen Elsa and Princess Anna were the happiest of all, for they had found their way back to each other!

Disney
FROZEN
CHILDHOOD TIMES

IT WAS A BEAUTIFUL day in the little kingdom of Arendelle. The Baron and Baroness of Snoob had just arrived for a visit. King Agnarr and Queen Iduna proudly welcomed their guests. If all went well, Arendelle would soon have a new trade partner.

Upstairs, Elsa and Anna stared at their breakfast in disbelief.

"We get chocolate just because we have visitors?" Anna asked.

"I suppose we *could* refuse to eat it," Elsa said, teasing her.

"No!" Anna chomped on her chocolate croissant. "Elsa, can we play with the magic?"

"We're supposed to stay in our rooms," Elsa said.

"Elsa, pleeeeease?" Anna begged.

"Okay!" Elsa agreed. "But we can't let them catch us!"

Together, the sisters snuck into the castle's grand hallway. The king and queen were still outside with their visitors, so Elsa raised her hands high in the air.

Whoosh! Glistening ice instantly covered the floors and railings.

"Whee!" Anna shouted as she slid across the floor.

"Anna, watch this!" Elsa said. With a wave of her arms, an icy rooster appeared—then a palm tree and a tiger!

Suddenly, the sisters heard the king and queen coming inside with the baron and baroness. They quickly slipped away. Luckily, nobody spotted them!

The king and queen led the tour directly into the hallway. Anna and Elsa were gone, but their ice sculptures were still in place.

"Ah! I say!" the Baron of Snoob exclaimed. "These statues are absolutely extraordinary!"

His wife, the baroness, was less impressed.

Carefully, the girls crept to the kitchen. With a mischievous grin, Elsa made huge amounts of snow and ice. Soon the sisters were having a big snowball fight.

"See that pan?" Elsa shouted, pointing behind her. She hit it with a snowball. "Woo-hoo!"

The two girls were having so much fun that they almost didn't see the king and queen arriving with their royal visitors. Quickly, Anna and Elsa headed up the back staircase.

When the king and queen entered the kitchen, they were surprised to see all the ice. But the baron thought the snowballs were wonderful.

"Oh, my. This is just what we need on a warm summer's day!" he exclaimed. "You must try it, my dear!"

"Harumph!" The baroness stared at her icy snow cone.

"Ah, yes!" the king said, chuckling. "Ice is Arendelle's number one product!"

"Indeed! We harvest lots of ice from lakes up in the nearby mountains," the queen added, not mentioning that her daughter sometimes helped.

There was no stopping the girls! Anna and Elsa ran through the rest of the castle leaving a trail of ice and snow behind them. In the ballroom, Elsa made snowy hills. Both girls slid up into the air and then down again. Together they raced around the ballroom. They even made snow angels!

Suddenly, the girls heard the guests approaching.

"Uh-oh!" Elsa said, startled. "We'd better hide!"

Giggling, the girls raced back to their bedroom.

"That was close!" Anna chirped. "They almost saw us!"

Meanwhile, down in the ballroom, the king and queen gasped when they saw the snowy hills and the—

"Oof!" The baroness slipped and landed in a pile of snow.

"Oh, dear," the queen said. She and the king rushed to help their guests.

"Snow angels!" the baroness cried out. "I love snow angels. What a delightful surprise!"

"I say." The baron chuckled. "The kingdom of Arendelle stops at nothing to please its visitors!"

After the visitors had
gone to their guest rooms
for the evening, the king and
queen went to check on their
daughters.

They found the sisters in
Elsa's bed. Both appeared to be
sleeping soundly.

The queen smiled. She knew
the girls had been very busy all
day.

As their parents turned
away, a small smile appeared
on Anna's face. She listened for
the sound of the door closing
and then popped upright.

Anna looked at her big sister. "Elsa do you want to play?" she asked.

"Anna, we can't! We're already going to be in a ton of trouble tomorrow," Elsa said.

Anna flopped back onto her pillow and sighed. "Still . . ."

"It was *so* worth it!" the girls said together.

DISNEY
FROZEN

OLAF'S PERFECT SUMMER DAY

SUMMER HAD FINALLY ARRIVED in Arendelle. Everyone in the kingdom was enjoying the long sunny days after a very cold winter. Kristoff and the other ice harvesters were on the docks, handing out ice to keep everyone cool. This was going to be the hottest day of the year so far!

Most of the villagers wanted to stay inside, where it was cool, but Olaf could hardly wait to get outside! This was the kind of summer day that he had always dreamed of!

"Anna! Anna!" Olaf called, running into the princess's room. "Guess what today is? It's the perfect summer day! Let's go outside and play. I bet there will be bees buzzing and dandelions fuzzing everywhere."

Anna groaned as she sat up in bed. It was sure to be hot and sticky outside! Then she saw Olaf's hopeful face. How could she say no?

Anna got dressed, and the two went to look for Elsa.

"There you are!" Olaf cried joyfully when they found her at last. "Today is exactly the kind of day I've been waiting for my whole snowman life. Please, can we go play in the sunshine?"

Elsa laughed. "That sounds like fun, Olaf," she said.

Olaf, Anna, and Elsa set off at once for their fun summer day.

In the royal gardens, they noticed some children lying on the grass. Giggling, Olaf bounded over to them.

"Hi, my name is Olaf. Don't you just love summer?"

The children were so charmed by Olaf that they jumped up and began to roll around in the grass.

Soon Olaf had all the children chasing butterflies. Summer was turning out to be exactly like he'd always imagined!

After a while, Anna plopped down on the grass.

"Whew! All that running and playing tired me out!" she said.

Elsa agreed. "Let's head to the docks. I think we can find a nice boat to sail to the fjord."

Olaf, who had been chasing a bumblebee, stopped in his tracks. "We're going sailing? I've always wanted to try sailing!"

At the docks, Anna and Elsa chose a beautiful sailboat. As they set sail, Olaf hummed happily. He even got to steer the boat.

When they reached the shore, Elsa set up the picnic basket. But Olaf couldn't sit still.

"Don't you just love the feeling of sand on your snow, Anna?" he squealed. "Come on! Let's make sand angels together!"

Anna gingerly stuck her toes into the hot sand. "Oh, goodness, that is . . . uh . . . warm," she squeaked.

She quickly danced on tiptoe to the fjord's edge. "Ah, this is better," she said as water washed over her feet.

The three friends spent the whole afternoon playing in the summer sun. They built sand castles and sand people, and they even danced with the seagulls!

As the sisters splashed around together in the water, Olaf chased the waves . . . and was then chased *by* them!

Finally, when they'd tired themselves out, Anna, Elsa, and Olaf had a picnic on the shores of the fjord.

Olaf held a cool glass of lemonade in his hands. He couldn't drink the tasty treat, but he enjoyed the feeling of the cool glass all the same. "Hands down, this has been the best day of my life," Olaf said with a happy smile.

As they sailed back to Arendelle, Olaf admired the beautiful colors the setting sun made in the sky.

"I wish I could hug the summer sun," he said. "I bet it would feel wonderful!"

Anna smiled tiredly. "You might need a bigger snow flurry for that, Olaf," she said.

Back at the docks, Kristoff and Sven had just returned from harvesting the mountain lakes. Their sled was once again full of ice.

Anna jumped out of the boat and flung herself against the deliciously cold blocks. "Oh, am I glad to see you!" she exclaimed.

Meanwhile, Olaf told Kristoff and Sven all about his adventures. When he finished, he sighed with happiness. "I wish it could always be summer!" he said.

Elsa smiled mischievously. "Summer is pretty wonderful," she said. "But for tomorrow, I predict a chance of snow!"

Disney
FROZEN

THE PERFECT BIRTHDAY

ANNA WAS EXCITED. TOMORROW was her fifth birthday. That was as many years as she had fingers on one hand! And that made it a very big birthday.

"Oh, I just can't wait!" Anna told her big sister, Elsa, as they got ready for bed. "It feels like it's taking forever for tomorrow to come!"

Just then, Anna and Elsa's mother came to tuck them into bed and say good night.

"You know," Queen Iduna told Anna, "the best way to make tomorrow come faster is to go to sleep. Then, when you wake up, it will be your big day."

Anna smiled as she crawled into bed. "Tell me again what it will be like," she said to her mother.

"Well," Queen Iduna said, "there will be a grand party, with fancy food and beautiful decorations and many important guests. And, of course, a pretty new dress for the birthday girl."

When Anna woke up the next morning, the first thing she saw was her birthday dress sitting in the corner of her room.

"Oooh," she breathed. "It's so fancy!" And it was. With embroidered trim and lace at the hem, it was the prettiest dress Anna had ever seen.

It was perfectly new, perfectly tailored, perfectly . . . perfect!

Anna ate a quick breakfast, and then Gerda helped her into her party dress.

When Anna stepped out of her room, she found Elsa waiting for her. It was time to get their hair done for the party.

"I'll race you there!" Anna cried.

Anna took off running, but she tripped over her own feet and got dust all over herself.

Elsa laughed at her sister and brushed the dress clean. "Come on! We're going to be late!"

Elsa took Anna's hand, and together the two sisters skipped down the hall.

"Birthday curls for the birthday girl!" their hairdresser said when Anna and Elsa arrived. "And braids for her big sister."

The hairdresser set to work. Soon Anna had a headful of little curls.

"Now don't move," the hairdresser told Anna sternly. "These have to set for one hour."

Anna made a face. How was she going to sit still for a whole hour?

"Want me to read you a story, Anna?" Elsa offered.

"Yes, please!" Anna said. It was hard, but with Elsa's story to focus on, Anna managed to sit still until her hair was finished.

Anna looked in the mirror. Her hair looked perfect! She spun around in a circle. As she did, a single curl came loose. Anna looked at herself again. Now she liked her hair even more!

Soon it was time for Anna's royal birthday party. "Wow," she whispered as she peeked into the banquet hall. There were so many people!

Anna knew that perfect manners were a must at a fancy party.

After all, she didn't want to embarrass her parents. So with a little wave at Elsa, Anna walked into the hall with her head held high. She nodded politely at each guest seated at the table.

And when she sat down, she made sure to sweep her skirt under her so it wouldn't crease.

Anna behaved perfectly all the way through dinner. She kept her elbows off the table, and she made sure to eat everything on her plate. Having perfect manners wasn't exactly fun, but Anna knew her parents would be proud of her.

It was all going great . . . until she let out a loud burp!

"Excuse me!" Anna said, clapping both hands over her mouth. Her cheeks turned red in embarrassment. Burping was *definitely* not good birthday manners.

Anna's father smiled. "Don't worry," he reassured Anna. "Sometimes a burp is a compliment to the chef!"

And then the king burped!

"There," he said. "Now the chef knows we *both* enjoyed the meal."

Anna laughed. Her father always knew how to make her feel better.

When the cake came, Anna tried her hardest to eat neatly, but she still ended up with frosting on her face. She crossed her eyes and tried not to giggle at the big, creamy blob on her nose.

But before Anna could do anything, her mother swiped the frosting off Anna's nose . . . and right into her own mouth!

"Yum!" she said, winking at Anna.

Anna couldn't help smiling.

That night as she got ready for bed, Anna sighed. She had really been looking forward to her birthday. But she'd been concentrating so hard on acting perfectly that she hadn't had a chance to have any fun!

Suddenly, Anna heard a voice: "Psst!" It was Elsa!

"Are you ready for your real party?" Elsa asked.

"My real party?" Anna responded. "Isn't that what I just had?"

With a grin, Elsa waved her hand. "Those royal parties are too proper to be any fun. The best way to celebrate is with a sisters-only party!"

Elsa grabbed Anna by the hand and pulled her into the hall. "There are just two rules," she said. "No manners, and no grown-ups."

Anna and Elsa snuck through the castle as quietly as they could. First the sisters raided the kitchen for leftover birthday cake, which they ate with their hands and no forks or plates!

Then they snuck into the laundry and took out as many pillows and blankets as they could carry. The two dragged their supplies back to their bedroom, where they built the biggest pillow fort Anna had ever seen! The sisters even had a pillow fight.

Just when Anna thought her night couldn't get any better, Elsa gave her a special birthday gift. It was a painting Elsa had made of the two of them. Anna loved it!

Much, much later, Anna and Elsa finally climbed into bed for the night.

"You were right," Anna said. "Sisters-only is way better."

"Did you have a good birthday?" Elsa asked.

"Thanks to you," Anna told her sister, "it was perfect."

FROZEN

ACROSS THE SEA

"THERE'S OUR SHIP, ELSA!" Anna exclaimed, peering out the window. "Are you almost ready?"

"Just about," Elsa replied as she packed the last of her things in her trunk. She smiled at her sister's impatience, but really, she couldn't wait to go on their trip, either.

For a few months, Elsa had been planning a royal tour to visit nearby kingdoms. And now it was time to leave! Her heart fluttered with excitement.

As the sisters climbed aboard their ship, the captain hurried over to them. He looked worried.

"Your Majesty," the captain said to Elsa, "I got the itinerary you sent. But I don't think we'll make it to the first stop on time. Not with waters this still."

"Don't worry," Anna said, taking the wheel.

"We've got it covered," Elsa said, creating a light snow flurry to push them along.

Soon the ship arrived at its first port: the kingdom of Zaria. The people clapped and cheered at the sight of their visitors.

"Welcome, Queen Elsa and Princess Anna!" King Stebor called in a booming voice as he met them at the dock.

"We cannot wait to show you our kingdom," Queen Renalia added warmly.

"Thank you!" Anna and Elsa said together, bowing gracefully to their hosts.

First the king and queen of Zaria invited the sisters to lunch, where Anna and Elsa enjoyed tasty new foods and lively conversation.

"Renalia thought I couldn't talk when we first met. I was so nervous around her," King Stebor told them.

"Oh, that's sweet!" Anna said.

"Yes, except now he won't stop talking," Queen Renalia said with a chuckle.

Next Anna and Elsa were taken on a tour of Zaria's prized gardens. Elsa pointed out a flower that looked like their friend Olaf.

"We'll be sure to send you home with some of those seeds," King Stebor said with a smile.

That night, the girls were treated to a grand festival.

"We've heard so much about your special talents," Queen Renalia said to Elsa. "Won't you show us some of your magic?"

Suddenly, Elsa felt shy. She nodded at the dance floor. "Would you like to join the dancing, Your Majesties?" she asked, changing the subject. "That looks like fun."

The next morning, Anna and Elsa set out for the kingdom of Chatho. The sisters met Chatho's ruler, Queen Colisa, in front of her impressive palace.

"Thank you for having us, Your Majesty," Elsa said.

"Of course," the queen responded warmly. "I am very happy you are both here!"

Queen Colisa took the sisters on a walk through the kingdom's rain forest, where they saw many unique animals.

Anna was particularly fond of some bashful furry creatures.

"Why, hello there!" she said, waving at the animals.

After their walk, the queen led Anna and Elsa into an enormous gallery. Chatho was known for its striking art and relics.

As Anna admired Chatho's treasures, Elsa spoke with the queen. "These are beautiful," she said.

"I'm so glad you think so," Queen Colisa replied. "Would you like to add a sculpture to our collection?"

Elsa noticed a block of ice under a spotlight, ready to be carved. Once again, she felt a wave of shyness.

Noticing her sister's discomfort, Anna jumped in. "Um . . . sure! Ice sculptures are actually my specialty!"

Soon it was time for the sisters to move on. As they got off their ship in the next kingdom, Anna asked Elsa why she didn't want to show off her powers.

"I guess I just got nervous," Elsa admitted.

Anna was about to reply when she spotted someone surprising walking toward them: the Duke of Weselton!

"What are you doing *here*?" Anna asked the Duke.

The sisters had purposefully avoided Weselton on their tour. Their last stop before home was the kingdom of Vakretta, which was far from Weselton.

The Duke smoothed his coat. "I am visiting my mother's cousin's wife's nephew, if you must know," he said. "Although I wish I weren't. If I were you, I would turn my ship around right now."

The sisters looked at each other, confused.

The Duke sighed. "Vakretta is having the hottest summer in years. Of course, you wouldn't care about *that*," he said, glaring at Elsa.

The sisters followed the Duke to the village. When they arrived,
they were surprised to see Vakrettans sprawled out, sweaty and tired.

For once, Elsa didn't feel shy. She knew she had to do something
to cool the people down. She quickly conjured some snow clouds,
much to the delight of the villagers. The snow was refreshing!

"It's working!" the Duke cried in surprise.

Elsa started making frosted mugs out of ice. "Why don't you get
us some lemonade?" she asked.

"Thank you, Queen Elsa! Thank you!" the crowd cheered.

Soon Vakretta was a frozen wonderland. Citizens built snow castles and ice-skated.

"I suppose a thank-you is in order," the Duke said. "I frankly don't know where to begin. . . ."

"Grab a board," Elsa suggested with a sly grin.

The Duke turned red and started sputtering. "A duke would never. . . ."

"It's okay. We'll show you how it's done," Anna called as she and Elsa grabbed some planks and slid down a hill.

A few hours later, it was time for Anna and Elsa to return to Arendelle. They waved to their new friends from the ship.

"Did you have a good trip?" Anna asked her sister.

"I did," Elsa replied as she created an icy blast of snow to direct them homeward. "I'd say it was the best royal tour ever . . . until next time, that is!"

Disney
FROZEN

BULDA'S CRYSTAL

KRISTOFF AND SVEN WERE visiting the trolls. They had come to help them harvest mushrooms while Grand Pabbie was away. Now, after a long day, they were relaxing by the campfire with Bulda and the other trolls.

As the fire began to fade, one of Bulda's crystals started to flicker. "Oh, no!" she said, surprised. "My crystal is going dark."

"Don't worry," said Kristoff. "You have plenty of others."

"Yes, but this is my favorite," Bulda said. "Grand Pabbie gave it to me when you first came to live with us."

Bulda looked down at her crystal. "When this type of crystal goes dark, it must be recharged by the next time the northern lights fade from the sky or its magical glow will be lost. Grand Pabbie would know how to do it, but he's not here."

Kristoff looked at Bulda. She had given him and Sven a home. He was grateful to her for so much, and he hated to see her disappointed. "Sven and I will fix your crystal," he said firmly.

As the sun began to rise, Kristoff and Sven set off for Arendelle. They found Anna, Elsa, and Olaf in the library.

"There's a book about crystals in here somewhere," Elsa suggested, grabbing a large dusty book. Quickly, she scanned the pages. "This says that troll crystals can be reenergized 'where lights wake the sky, where sky touches the earth, and where waters run long.'"

"Lights that wake up the sky could be the northern lights," Kristoff said. "And 'where sky touches the earth' could be a mountaintop."

"There's a long, narrow fjord by Opplading Mountain," Anna said. "I bet that's 'where waters run long'!"

Opplading Mountain was a full day's journey from Arendelle. The friends quickly packed food, blankets, and a map and set out on their quest.

The group had been hiking all morning when they arrived at the top of a steep cliff. Kristoff looked over the side, searching for a trail to follow.

"According to the map, we'll have to climb down the cliff," Anna said. "There's no other way around."

Olaf peeked over the cliff. "Wow!" His eyes grew wide. Then he laughed. "Let's go!"

Kristoff smiled. "You might want to use a rope! Just go slow and you'll be fine."

Anna smiled and lowered herself over the cliff. "This should be fun!"

"Is Anna going slow enough?" Olaf asked as Anna bounced down the cliff face.

"Well, maybe going slowly isn't as important as going carefully," Kristoff said with a smile.

"I don't think the climbing part is necessary," Elsa said with a sly smile. "I have an easier way."

With a wave of her hand, Elsa used her magic to create an ice slide down the side of the cliff! Then she, Olaf, and Sven slid past Kristoff and Anna. But when the friends got to the bottom of the cliff, they found another cliff to climb up!

After hours of walking along the fjord and climbing up and down hills, the group finally reached the top of Opplading Mountain. To their surprise, nothing was at the summit except bare rocks and large boulders. They looked around, puzzled. Where were the crystals?

The sun was beginning to set, so the group decided to stop for the night. "Maybe we'll have better luck in the morning," Anna said.

The friends set up camp under a rocky overhang. As they settled into their blankets, Kristoff sang a new song he had written. Suddenly, a ribbon of glowing color spread across the night sky.

"I love it when the sky's awake," Olaf said, sighing happily. "But I've never seen the rocks glow."

Everyone turned to see what Olaf was looking at. Where the light from the colorful sky hit the rocks above them, they could see spots of red, green, yellow, and purple glowing deep inside the boulders!

"Could those be crystals?" Elsa asked.

Kristoff ran his hands over the rock. He took out his climbing ax, but Sven nudged him out of the way.

The reindeer backed up and charged at the rock. His antlers hit it with a loud *BOOM!*

Unfortunately, the sound was more impressive than the tiny cracks that appeared in the rock.

"Maybe I can help," Elsa said. She waved her hand, summoning her powers so that ice formed against the wall and crept into the cracks. The freezing rock forced the cracks wider apart and a small hole appeared.

Seeing her chance, Anna wriggled her hand inside. She didn't get far. "It's too tight," she cried.

"Uh-oh," Elsa said. "The lights in the sky are starting to fade—and the crystals in the rock are, too!"

Anna thought for a moment. "Maybe there's another way. Kristoff, may I see Bulda's crystal?"

Anna reached into the rock again, this time holding Bulda's darkened crystal. As the crystals touched, a magical charge passed between them. Bulda's crystal began to glow again!

The friends cheered. They had restored Bulda's crystal. But as dawn broke, the illuminated crystal began to fade.

"What's happening?" Anna asked.

"I thought we had successfully completed the quest!" Elsa said, shaking her head.

"I guess we had the wrong mountain," Kristoff said sadly.

The friends packed their things and headed back down the mountain toward Arendelle.

They were upset that they hadn't been able to recharge Bulda's crystal, but they knew they'd tried their best.

That night, back in Troll Valley, Bulda greeted the group of friends with big hugs.

"We weren't able to recharge your crystal," Kristoff admitted sadly to Bulda. "I'm so sorry."

"Well, this crystal can be finicky," Bulda said with a smile. "Let's take a look."

"Here you go," said Anna. The crystal looked dull and faded in her hands.

The friends gathered together as Anna placed the crystal in Bulda's hands.

Suddenly, the crystal began to glow brightly!

"You see?" Bulda said. "You had a challenge, and you worked together to overcome it. The powerful charge of friendship and family provided the last bit of special energy the crystal needed to glow bright again."

Kristoff grinned. "I get it! But don't forget that we did it for you, because you're family, too."

As Bulda pulled them in for a group hug, they all had to agree that family and friendship were two of the most powerful forces in the world.

IT WAS EARLY MORNING in the kingdom of Arendelle, and Queen Elsa was hard at work. It was Anna's birthday—the first the sisters had spent together since they were children. Elsa wanted it to be Anna's best birthday ever!

Elsa waved her hands, and a small ice sculpture appeared on the cake she had made for Anna. It was pretty, but it didn't seem quite right. With a flick of her wrist, she tried again.

Behind her, Kristoff was working on a birthday banner. It read HAPPY BIRTHDAY ANNA in big drippy letters.

Elsa looked at the messy banner. "Kristoff, are you sure I can leave you in charge here?" she asked.

Suddenly, the kingdom bells began to chime. Like it or not, Elsa would have to trust Kristoff to finish the party preparations.

Elsa took a deep breath and hurried through the castle to Anna's bedroom. She found her sister fast asleep.

"*Psst*. Anna. Happy birthday!" she whispered softly.

Anna yawned sleepily and stretched. "It's my birthday," she mumbled.

As Anna realized what she had just said, she sat up, fully awake.

"It's my birthday!" she shouted excitedly.

Elsa smiled at her sister. "And it's going to be perfect!"

Then Elsa gave Anna her first birthday present: a beautiful new green-and-teal dress. With a wave of her hand, Elsa used her magic to add icy sparkles to the dress. Then she picked up some flowers from a nearby vase. With a flick of her wrist, she frosted the flowers onto her own gown.

Suddenly, Elsa sneezed.

"ACHOO!"

"Bless you!" Anna said.

Unseen by Anna and Elsa, two tiny snowmen appeared. Elsa had accidentally created them with her sneeze! The tiny snowmen dropped to the floor and scampered off.

"Thanks, Sis," Elsa said, sniffing and rubbing her nose. "Now come on, you have a birthday to enjoy."

Smiling, she handed the end of a string to Anna. "Just follow the string!" she said.

Anna held on to the string and followed her older sister out of the room.

Anna eagerly followed the string down the halls and over and under furniture. With each stop on the string, she found a birthday present! There was a beautiful bracelet, a silly Olaf cuckoo clock, and even a giant painting of the sisters and all their friends.

Elsa really *had* thought of everything! There was only one problem: her sneezing seemed to be getting worse and worse.

Elsa sneezed and sneezed. With each sneeze, more mini snowmen appeared. The snowgies happily scurried off, unnoticed by the sisters.

Out in the courtyard, Kristoff, Sven, and Olaf were keeping an eye on the surprise party.

Just then, Olaf heard a noise. "Hello . . . ?" he called.

The little snowmen created by Elsa's sneezes crashed into the courtyard. They raced around, knocking over party decorations!

Kristoff chased the snowmen. He couldn't let them destroy Anna's party! Olaf, on the other hand, was very excited. He hugged the snowmen close. "Little brothers!" he cried happily.

Inside the castle, Anna's birthday adventure continued. Anna was having a wonderful time, but she could tell Elsa wasn't feeling well.

Soon the birthday string led them out of the castle to the Oaken's Cloakens and Sauna kiosk in the marketplace. As Elsa sneezed again, Oaken popped out of the sauna. He offered Elsa a cold medicine of his own making.

Anna eagerly accepted the medicine. "We'll take it!" she said.

Elsa was beginning to feel dizzy. But she still had one gift left to give Anna! And it was at the top of Arendelle's clock tower.

The sisters climbed up, up, up.

"Elsa, that's too much. You need to rest!" Anna said.

But Elsa insisted. At the very top, she gave Anna two beautiful wooden dolls. They looked just like the sisters—the perfect birthday present!

Suddenly, Elsa's cold got the better of her and she swooned. Anna dropped her presents to keep her sister from falling off the tower.

"Elsa, look at you. You've got a fever," Anna said, worried. "You're burning up!"

"I'm sorry, Anna," Elsa said sadly. "I just wanted to give you one perfect birthday."

Over in the courtyard, things were *not* going well. The snowgies were causing chaos. One group pulled down Kristoff's banner while a second group headed for the birthday cake. Thinking quickly, Kristoff grabbed Olaf's head and rolled it like a bowling ball toward the tower of snowmen.

But Kristoff was not fast enough. The snowgies were preparing to launch themselves at Anna's birthday cake!

"No, no, no!" Kristoff shouted as he reached for a bowl. He blocked them as they flew at the cake!

Meanwhile, Olaf grabbed the birthday banner and tried to rearrange all the letters in the right order. But he didn't know how to spell.

Kristoff read the new banner. "'Dry Banana Hippy Hat'?" he cried.

It was a disaster!

115

Anna led Elsa back to the castle. As they entered the courtyard, Elsa saw Kristoff, Olaf, and Sven trying to keep the cake away from the snowgies. Kristoff jumped up onto Sven, and Olaf ran by with the banner.

Anna didn't notice, but Elsa was horrified. It was chaos!

Anna looked up just as Kristoff caught the cake and the birthday banner settled into place. Her face lit up. To her, everything looked perfect! But where had all the little snowmen come from?

Kristoff hopped off Sven and walked up to Anna, birthday cake in hand. "Happy birthday," he said. "I love you, baby." For a minute he looked embarrassed. Then he shrugged. "I do."

Anna couldn't believe it. It was all so wonderful! But she was still worried about Elsa.

Elsa promised she was well enough for at least one piece of cake.

Sven cut slices for everyone. Then, finally, Anna led Elsa inside.

Upstairs, Anna tucked a very tired Elsa into bed. Anna made Elsa some hot soup, sat down next to her, and smiled. "Best birthday present ever," she told her sister as she fed her soup.

Elsa was confused. "Which one?" she asked.

"You letting me take care of you," Anna replied with a smile.

Anna's party was over, but Kristoff and Olaf still had one important thing left to do. Up in the mountains, they knocked on the doors to the ice palace. The doors swung open. Marshmallow was inside.

Olaf pushed past the giant snowman and ran into the palace. Behind him was a trail of little snowgies.

Kristoff sighed and looked at Marshmallow. "Don't ask."

Disney
FROZEN

A Royal Sleepover

"P**SSSSST! ELSA?**"
ANNA NUDGED
her sleeping sister.
"Come on, wake up."

Elsa shifted, groggy. "Go
back to bed, Anna. It's the
middle of the night," she said.

"I can't sleep!" Anna
flopped down on Elsa's bed.

Then Anna smiled slyly to
herself. She knew how to get
Elsa out of bed. "Wanna have
a sleepover?"

This time, Elsa opened
her eyes and grinned. That
sounded like a lot of fun!

While Anna went to her room to find extra pillows and blankets, Elsa headed to the kitchen to get the ingredients for her famous honey cones. After all, a sleepover wasn't a sleepover without snacks!

When Elsa got back to her room, she found Anna digging through the closet. She was looking for something.

"Aha!" Anna cried. "I knew it was here!"

Anna held up an old worn book. Her parents had read it to the sisters every night when they were little.

"Let's see, we've got books, games, and this face cream Oaken gave me the last time I went to the trading post," Anna said. She opened the cream. "It looks kinda . . . goopy."

Elsa laughed. "Let's save that for later!"

Elsa looked around. It had been a long time since she'd had a sleepover. "Sooo . . . what should we do first?" she asked.

Anna was ready. "How about we build a fort, like when we were kids?" she suggested.

Anna stacked pillows and blankets around the room, making lookouts and hidden caves. Meanwhile, Elsa created icy tunnels and snowy turrets.

"This is fun," Elsa said, putting the finishing touches on an icy archway. "I think we should add a—"

SMACK! Elsa felt something soft and feathery hit her back. She turned to see a fallen pillow and a giggling Anna.

"Oh, no you don't!" Elsa yelled, launching a snowball at her sister. Anna ducked, squealing in delight.

Before long, the room was covered in snow flurries and feathers. Anna was zooming down an icy slide on the fort when the sisters heard a knock at the door.

"Is it daytime already?" a familiar voice asked.

"Olaf!" Anna cried. The sisters welcomed their snowman friend inside.

Elsa explained that they were having a sleepover and invited Olaf to join them.

"A sleepover?" Olaf asked, excited. "Oh, I've always wanted to have one of those." He paused. "What's a sleepover?"

"We'll show you," Anna said. "Come on! I bet you'll be great at Pick-Up Sticks!"

Anna was right. Olaf was a natural at the fun game.

Anna was great at Work of Art. She guessed the drawing and sculpture every time!

Charades proved to be a bit more challenging. Olaf twisted his body this way and that, making frantic gestures and grinning widely. The sisters didn't know what the answer could be. Finally, Elsa had an idea.

"Olaf, are you acting out 'summer'?" she asked.

"Yes!" he cried. "You're good at this!"

Elsa laughed. "Maybe it's time to do something else," she said. "How about a scary story?"

Anna went first, using her spookiest, most dramatic voice. She even held a candle up to her face, casting eerie shadows on the wall behind her. "According to legend, the Hairy Hooligan only comes out on nights like these, looking for his next victim," she said.

"How do you know when the Hairy Hooligan is around?" Olaf asked.

"He lets out a low moan," Anna answered.

"*OOOOOOOHHHHH.*" A sad whine echoed through the room.

"Wow. That's really scary, Anna," Olaf said, impressed.

"Uh . . ." Anna blinked. "That wasn't me."

"*OOOOOOOOHHHHH!*" The cry sounded like it was coming from outside the castle.

A sudden noise made them all jump. Elsa, Anna, and Olaf ran to the window. A shadowy figure was walking toward them!

"Stay here," Elsa said, running down the hall. But Anna and Olaf followed. They couldn't let Elsa face the Hairy Hooligan alone!

Elsa opened the castle door, and the friends peered into the darkness. Olaf held Anna's hand, bracing himself for the Hairy Hooligan's pointed teeth and sharp claws.

But it wasn't a monster after all. It was Sven!

"Sven!" Elsa called out. "What's the matter?"

Anna took one look at the reindeer and guessed what was going on. "You couldn't sleep, could you, Sven?" She patted him gently on the nose. "I bet Kristoff is snoring and keeping you awake. The trolls said his snores are loud enough to start an avalanche!"

Sven nodded.

"You should come to our sleepover!" Olaf said. "From what I can tell, there's very little sleeping involved."

Soon the group was happily settled in Elsa's room.

Anna got Sven and Olaf to try the face cream from Oaken, and they all laughed as the goop slid down their chins. "How about another story?" Elsa suggested, holding up a book.

"Excellent!" Anna agreed. She fluffed some pillows, and she, Olaf, and Sven got comfortable as Elsa began reading.

A little while later, Elsa finished the story. She looked around, hearing the sounds of heavy breathing around her. The rest of the slumber party had fallen asleep!

Smiling, Elsa put down the book. She gently tucked in Anna, Olaf, and Sven and climbed into bed. Then, with one last look at Anna and her friends, Elsa, too, drifted off to sleep.

Disney FROZEN

A Cool Contest

*P*RINCESS ANNA LOOKED AROUND the courtyard. "It's the perfect day for the annual ice-carving contest," she told her sister, Queen Elsa. "Cold and clear and bright."

Elsa smiled. She had loved this contest when she was younger. Now that the castle gates were open again, she was thrilled to bring back the tradition. Ice harvesters had dragged large blocks of ice into the castle courtyard so the contestants could carve their creations. And from the large crowd, it seemed as if almost everyone in Arendelle was taking part in the contest.

Olaf ran up to the sisters. The little snowman tugged on Anna's dress. "Come on, Anna," he said. "Let's find our ice!"

"Okay," Anna said with a laugh. "See you later, Elsa!"

"Good luck," Elsa called as Olaf took Anna by the hand. They picked up some carving tools and made their way to their block of ice.

Nearby, Kristoff and Sven were admiring their own block of ice.

"I know this is my first time *sculpting* ice," Kristoff said, "but I've been cutting blocks of ice since I was a kid. How hard could it be?"

Sven nodded.

"We work with ice every day," Kristoff said. "We know the secrets of the ice. I know we'll make a great sculpture!"

Just then, Elsa clapped her hands.

"Good morning, everyone!" she said. "Welcome to the ice-carving contest!"

The crowd cheered.

"The rules are simple," Elsa said. "Carvers may either work alone or in teams of two. Each team will have until the sun sets to finish their sculpture. Then I will choose the winners. You may now begin. Good luck, everyone!"

As the carvers took their places, Anna saw Kristoff and Sven. Their block of ice was right next to hers and Olaf's!

"I didn't know you were entering the contest," she said to Kristoff.

"I didn't know you were entering, either," Kristoff replied.

"I guess I should have known," Anna said with a smile. "After all, ice is your life."

Kristoff laughed. He couldn't disagree with that!

Anna held out her hand. "Good luck," she said.

"May the best artist win!" Kristoff replied.

144

Anna and Olaf picked up their tools and together began chipping away at the ice. Anna leaned back and struck the ice with her chisel.

"Whoa! That was so much fun!" Anna said, taking another swing at the ice.

Olaf giggled with delight as he took a chip out of the block with his chisel. "This *is* fun! I wonder what it is we're making!"

"I guess we'll find out," Anna shouted as she happily hammered away at their block, sending ice chips spraying into the air all around them.

Meanwhile, Kristoff and Sven carefully searched their block of ice for lines and cracks. Kristoff put his ear to the ice and closed his eyes.

"Okay, Sven. Now I know where the ice will break!" Kristoff said finally.

Nearby, Anna saw Kristoff and Sven carefully start to carve their ice. She stopped and looked down at her own block of ice. She and Olaf had been having so much fun chipping away that their ice didn't look like anything. Maybe Kristoff had the right idea.

Anna and Olaf stopped carving and put down their tools. Kneeling, Anna tried to listen to the ice.

"What's it saying, Anna?" Olaf asked.

"I don't hear anything," Anna said. But then she noticed all the small lines and cracks in the ice. Now she knew where the ice would break! The friends picked up their tools and merrily started chipping away again.

The pair's laughter caught Kristoff's attention. Although their sculpture looked a little funny, Anna and Olaf seemed to be having a good time.

Kristoff looked at Sven and their block of ice. They had barely made a dent in it.

"Maybe we don't need to be so careful," Kristoff told Sven. "And I think I know just what we should carve."

He whispered something in Sven's ear. The reindeer smiled. Then the two of them got back to work. Kristoff used his chisel, and Sven used the sharp points of his antlers. Soon they were laughing, too.

As the hours ticked by, all the teams worked hard on their sculptures. Soon many of the sculptures began to take shape. One team was carving a dolphin. Another was working on a sculpture of an ocean bird. Kristoff and Sven slowly worked on their creation, while Anna and Olaf kept chipping away as quickly as they could.

Anna couldn't believe how much fun she was having. Ice carving might be her new hobby!

Finally, Elsa's voice rang out through the courtyard.

"The sun is setting!" she said. "It's time for the judging to begin."

Elsa walked up and down the rows, looking at each team's carving. One of the ice harvesters had carved a cute polar bear cub.

"That's wonderful!" said Elsa.

Then she looked at Kristoff and Sven's sculpture. She smiled.

"It looks like Sven! What a good idea," she said. "It's too bad you weren't able to finish."

Next Elsa moved to Anna and Olaf's sculpture.

"Well, you finished your sculpture," she said. "But what is it?"

"Can't you tell?" Olaf asked. "It's an ice man!"

"Oh, of course," Elsa said politely to Anna and Olaf. "It's . . . it's wonderful!"

Elsa moved from team to team, looking at the rest of the sculptures. She saw a fish, a dolphin, and a seagull. She saw a cat, a swan, and a sailing ship. There were many beautiful sculptures to choose from. It was going to be hard for Elsa to pick just one winner.

Finally, she stopped at Olina and Kai's sculpture. They had carved the castle.

Elsa couldn't believe her eyes. "It's beautiful!" she cried. "Just look at this detail. You've carved every window, every tower, and every brick!"

Elsa turned to the crowd. "Olina and Kai are the winners!" she announced, placing a ribbon on their sculpture.

As the crowd erupted into applause, Olina and Kai smiled proudly.

"You know," Kristoff told Anna, "I bet we could make something great if we had the right team."

Anna grinned. "Maybe next time we all can work together," she said. "You can listen to the ice."

"And you can make sure Sven and I don't get too serious," Kristoff added.

The two friends shook hands. They couldn't wait until the next contest!

FROZEN

KRISTOFF'S BIRTHDAY BASH

KRISTOFF LOVED LIVING WITH the trolls. One day, Kristoff and Sven noticed some trolls having a party.

"What are they celebrating?" Kristoff asked Bulda, his adoptive mother.

Bulda laughed. "Haven't you ever seen a century party before?" she asked. "It's to celebrate being another hundred years older! Today Morba is two centuries old!"

"Oh!" Kristoff said. "Like a birthday! Right, Sven?"

Bulda clapped her hands excitedly. "Humans have century parties, too?" she asked.

Sven snorted and shook his head.

"Well, not exactly," Kristoff said. "Humans celebrate their birthdays every year."

"Every year?" Bulda asked. "Why, that must mean our Kristoff has a birthday celebration coming up!"

Kristoff shrugged. "I don't actually know when my birthday is. Usually your family keeps track of that sort of thing, but . . ." His voice trailed off.

"But until you came to us, you had no family," Bulda finished gently. She gave her son a big hug. "Well, all that has changed. We'll just choose a day and declare it your birthday! Now what exactly goes on at a birthday party?"

Kristoff shrugged again. "I don't know, I've never been to one."

"I guess we'll just make it up as we go," Bulda said. "And we'll start by making it a surprise party!"

"But I already know about it," Kristoff said.

"Pish tosh," Bulda said. "That's a minor thing. Surprise party it is!"

That night, as Kristoff drifted to sleep beneath the bright moon, he couldn't stop smiling. A birthday party!

He never thought he'd have a birthday party, let alone a party with family.

When Kristoff woke up, he found that everyone in the valley had suddenly become very busy. They were too busy to play with him— or even talk to him!

"Hey, guys," Kristoff called out to some of his friends as they bustled by. "Do you want to—"

But before he could finish, they had disappeared around a corner.

He tried again. "Bulda, can we—" but she just waved and smiled and hurried off.

Kristoff looked around. Everyone seemed to be heading in the same direction. Suddenly, Kristoff realized what was happening.

"So, when's my surprise party?" he asked one troll.

"No idea what you're talking about," the troll said. "I don't even know who you are. What's a party, anyway? No such thing. *This conversation never happened.*"

"Oooookay," Kristoff said. "Well, at least I've still got Sven."

But when he turned around Sven had disappeared, too!

A few days later, Kristoff awoke to a loud "SURPRISE!"

Every troll in the valley had come to celebrate his birthday!

Kristoff had never seen so many trolls in one place before. They all looked at him expectantly.

"Well, are you surprised?" Bulda asked her son.

"Er . . . not really," Kristoff admitted. "But I am really, really happy!"

The trolls wasted no time. They pulled Kristoff from bed, got him dressed, and headed off to begin the party. The first activity was a rousing game of troll-bowling.

"What's that?" Kristoff asked.

"We all roll! Aim for the pinecones!" Bulda explained, whizzing by down the hill. "Wheee!"

Grinning, Kristoff leaped into the air and rolled himself down the hill after Bulda.

Kristoff spent the whole night playing games with his friends. The trolls had thought of everything. They had even made a special birthday dessert—mud pie!

Kristoff was skeptical at first, but he didn't want to let his family down. Squeezing his eyes closed, he took a small bite. It was delicious!

Suddenly, Bulda tugged on Kristoff's sleeve. "I bet my bat is faster than yours!" she said.

Kristoff was confused. "Bat?" he asked. "What bat?"

"For the bat races, of course!" Bulda said. "Everyone picks a bat, and we see which one gets to the gnat swarm first!"

The trolls chose their bats and released them into the air. Bulda was right. Her bat *was* faster than Kristoff's!

As the bats flew away, the trolls gathered around Kristoff. Each of them had come up with a brand-new story to tell in honor of Kristoff's birthday.

Kristoff listened happily to each of the stories. He couldn't believe his friends had gone to all this trouble just for him.

Later, Bulda tucked Kristoff into his mossy bed. "Did you have a good birthday party?" she asked.

"Best ever," Kristoff said sleepily. He gave Bulda a hug.

"I had fun, too," she said. "You know, human birthday parties are so much fun—we should do this again next year!"

Kristoff smiled. "I think that's the idea," he said.

And with that, he fell asleep, dreaming of spending many more birthdays with his new family.

Disney
FROZEN

OAKEN'S INVENTION

IGH IN THE MOUNTAINS above Arendelle was a special store—Wandering Oaken's Trading Post and Sauna. Oaken loved his store. He loved helping his customers and he loved his sauna. But most of all, he loved inventing new things that people might enjoy.

The only thing Oaken loved more than inventing things was spending time with his family. The next day was the biannual Oaken family reunion. His family would be coming from all over the different parts of Arendelle to visit his shop! Oaken was really excited to see everyone.

The Oaken family reunion was always fun. Oaken's aunts and uncles gobbled up lutefisk and lingonberry pie while his cousins played Reindeer Ringtoss and made snow angels. The whole family enjoyed participating in the Polar Plunge, followed by a nice warm steam in Oaken's sauna.

But the best part of the reunion was the Creator's Contest, when Oaken's family members shared the wonderful contraptions they had invented since the last family reunion. It was always full of surprises.

The Creator's Contest was usually Oaken's favorite family tradition, but this year he had a problem. He didn't have a new invention to show! Oaken felt bad. He didn't want to let his family down.

The shopkeeper was so lost in thought that he didn't even notice when the shop's bell jangled and Kristoff walked in.

Oaken didn't call out his usual greeting, so Kristoff tried it himself. "Hoo-hoo!" he called. "Ice delivery!"

Startled, Oaken looked up. "Hoo-hoo," he said gloomily.

"What's wrong, Oaken?" Kristoff asked.

Oaken sighed. "I haven't invented anything for my family's Creator's Contest tomorrow."

"Inventing can be a tough business," Kristoff said. "But sometimes inspiration can come from the most unexpected places."

Oaken nodded, but he wasn't sure he agreed with the ice harvester.

"Don't worry about it, Oaken," Kristoff said as he walked toward the door. "I'm sure you'll think of something!"

After Kristoff left, Oaken tried to think of an invention. But none of his ideas seemed special enough for the Creator's Contest. Finally, he decided to take a break in his sauna. A hot steam might clear his mind and help him think.

As Oaken made his way toward the sauna, he tripped over the stack of ice blocks Kristoff had delivered. One of the blocks slid toward a clearing in the trees.

As it came to rest, the edges of the ice started to glow a soft silver. Curious, Oaken walked to the ice block.

As he approached the block, Oaken saw the colors from the northern lights glinting through the ice, causing it to glow. Suddenly, Oaken had an idea. He knew exactly what to invent for the Creator's Contest. Oaken picked up the ice and raced back to his shop. He didn't have a moment to waste!

The next day, Oaken's family arrived. Everyone was happy to see one another. "Hoo-hoo!" each one called out in greeting. The adults ate krumkake while the children raced their sleds. Finally, after a day of games and activities, it was time for the Creator's Contest. The family gathered around to see what wonderful new inventions their relatives had come up with.

Grandma Hedda held up a sweater that had earmuffs attached to the neck with a string.

Cousin Agathe played her newest composition on her Hardanger fiddle. Some of the family appreciated that more than others.

At long last, it was Oaken's turn. "Follow me, family," he sang out.

Excited, Oaken's family followed him. "What could he possibly have made?" they wondered.

"I hope whatever it is will be as good as the shoes for walking on snow," Aunt Klara said.

Oaken led his family into the clearing. Standing by itself in the middle of the trees was an enormous block of ice.

"That's a nice big block of ice ya got there, Oaken," Cousin Lars said. "But what does it do?"

"You'll see," Oaken said, putting out the fire on his torch. Everything went black. Oaken's family looked around, confused.

Just then, the northern lights appeared in the sky! As their light hit the block of ice, bright bursts of color erupted everywhere, sparkling on the trees, against the snow, and across the faces of the astonished Oaken clan.

Oaken beamed proudly.

"It's a lantern for the temporary capturing of polar lights," he explained, pointing to the sky. "For the celebrating of special moments, like Oaken family reunions."

Oaken's family was astonished. It was beautiful! Everyone
agreed that Oaken had the best invention. He was the winner of the
Creator's Contest. Oaken was delighted to have won, but he had
realized something. Spending time with his family was the best
prize of all!

DISNEY
FROZEN

Elsa's (Surprise) Surprise Party

ONE BRIGHT WINTER MORNING, Queen Elsa woke up with the strangest feeling that she was forgetting something important.

What could it be? Elsa wondered. She wasn't late for any appointments. She'd already prepared her remarks for her lunch with the lichen farmers that day. And she'd even remembered to approve the menu for the following week's ball.

Suddenly, Elsa gasped. *Today's my birthday!* she realized. *How could I have forgotten?*

Elsa checked her schedule. Birthday or no birthday, she had a lot to do! *Maybe Anna will forget, too,* she thought. *Then I won't have to go to a party.* After such a busy day, it would be nice to just unwind with family and friends. If Anna remembered Elsa's birthday, she'd probably plan some big event with lots of people.

But it was clear when Elsa entered the dining room for breakfast that her friends had not forgotten.

Anna jumped up and gave Elsa a big hug "for no reason." And Kristoff had made special pancakes "just because."

Suddenly, the royal butler appeared with a note for Anna.

"This must be about the flowers," Anna said, quickly clapping her hands over her mouth. "I mean the *towers*," she said. "You know . . . the ones we're adding to the south wing."

"This castle doesn't have a south wing," Elsa pointed out.

"It does now!" Anna said as she headed to the door. "I really should go check on this. Bye!"

A few minutes later, Olina entered the dining room.

"Pardon me," she said to Kristoff, "but the royal baker asked me to tell you that he can't manage fifty cake layers."

Kristoff shook his head. "Cake? What cake? There's no cake," he said nervously. "Fifty *players* is what he meant. For the, uh, chess tournament that's happening today."

Kristoff turned awkwardly to Elsa. "Um, I better go talk to the baker about this cake—I mean, tournament—right away."

Elsa smirked as she watched Kristoff leave the dining room. She knew very well that there was no chess tournament that day.

"Kristoff must really love chess," Olaf said cheerfully, interrupting her thoughts. "What is chess? Here, have some more pancakes. The syrup is so sticky and fun!"

Elsa smiled and shook her head. Olaf might not know what was going on, but she wasn't fooled. Anna and Kristoff were obviously planning a surprise birthday party for her . . . and it was clearly going to be big. Large parties weren't Elsa's favorite, but it was nice that Anna and Kristoff cared enough about her birthday to plan one.

Elsa put her birthday—and her surprise party—out of her mind and headed to the throne room. She had a busy morning ahead of her, hearing requests and offering advice to the people of Arendelle.

"I have too many dogs," the first of her subjects said. "I need to find a new home for one of them."

"I need to find a dog so I can herd sheep," remarked the second of Elsa's subjects.

"I need to hire a sheepherder for my flock," the third said.

Elsa thought for a moment and then smiled. "I think I see a good solution," she said.

Next Elsa moved on to lunch with the group of lichen farmers who were visiting from the northernmost region of Arendelle.

"We brought you a traditional northern Arendelle delicacy," one farmer said, holding out a green cookie for Elsa to try. She took a small bite and tried not to make a face. It tasted horrible!

"It's made out of lichen," another farmer explained.

"It's certainly unique," Elsa said politely. "I'm honored."

After lunch, Elsa sat down to review the royal budget. Suddenly, a messenger raced in with an urgent letter. There had been a landslide in a nearby village. No one had been hurt, but several of the villagers were trapped in their homes.

Elsa knew just who to ask for help. She quickly wrote a letter and handed it to the messenger.

"Take this to the captain of the guard, please," she said. "And hurry."

Elsa knew the captain had many strong men. They would be able to free the villagers in no time.

Elsa sighed. Landslides were dangerous, but budgets could be boring!

As day turned to dusk, Elsa looked out over Arendelle. Usually evening was her favorite time of day. She would have a quiet dinner with Anna and Kristoff, then read by the fire or take a walk with Olaf. She always looked forward to it.

But that night Elsa knew she would have to be more social. Her "surprise" party was probably going to have five hundred guests and a cake the size of a reindeer.

They're doing this because they love you, Elsa reminded herself. *And at least Anna will have a good time. Anna loves big parties.*

At that moment, Anna appeared in the doorway.

"Elsa," she said casually, "what a coincidence. I was just looking for you. I need you to come have a look at the new . . . uh . . . towers."

Elsa couldn't help smiling. "The new towers," she repeated.

Anna led Elsa through the castle in awkward silence. Finally, Elsa took pity on her younger sister.

"You don't have to pretend, Anna" she said, stopping in front of the doors to the ballroom. "I know you're throwing me a huge surprise party."

Anna gave her sister a sly smile. "Oh, it's a surprise, all right," she said. "Just not the way you think."

201

Anna threw open the doors.

Elsa had been right. Inside was a giant cake! But everything else was a complete—

"SURPRISE!" Anna and Kristoff shouted.

"It's your birthday!" yelled Olaf.

Elsa looked around in astonishment. "I can hardly believe it," she said. She was amazed!

"Me neither," Olaf agreed, shaking his head. "But this actually explains a lot. Like the cake and all the presents."

Elsa couldn't believe her eyes. There was no string quartet, no fancy china, no crowd of hundreds of guests. . . .

"It's just us," Anna said. "A quiet little party with your family and friends."

"Just what I wanted," Elsa said, hugging her sister.

"So were you surprised?" Anna asked later.

"Very!" Elsa said with a smile. "I thought for sure you were planning a huge bash. You love giant parties."

"But you don't," Anna said. "You love quiet evenings with your family and your best friends. And on your birthday, you should get exactly what you want."

Disney FROZEN

A New Friend

SPRING HAD FINALLY SPRUNG in Arendelle. Olaf was enjoying the warm air when he saw Queen Elsa and Princess Anna walking toward him. "Hi, Anna! Hi, Elsa!" he called. "Where are you going?"

Anna smiled at the snowman. "It's such a nice day we thought we'd take a walk," she said. "Wanna come?"

Olaf couldn't believe his luck. A whole day with Anna and Elsa! Nodding, he hurried after the sisters.

The trio hadn't been walking long before they came upon Wandering Oaken's Trading Post and Sauna.

"Ooh, a sauna!" Olaf said. "That sounds nice."

Anna giggled. "I'm not sure that's such a good idea," she told the snowman. "But Oaken's store is always fun to look around. Come on, Elsa. Let's go inside and say hi!"

Anna had first met Oaken when she was looking for Elsa on the North Mountain. Now, she liked to visit his store whenever she had time. Grabbing Elsa by the arm, Anna pulled her sister inside.

"Hoo-hoo!" called Oaken as the girls entered the trading post. "Big winter blowout sale!"

"Hi, Oaken!" Anna said. "Do you have anything special for us today?"

Oaken nodded and reached behind him. "These shoes for walking on snow are special. And that sled for sliding down mountains. Half off!" he said. "Sweaters are also two for one!"

Anna grinned. How could she possibly say no to a great offer like *that*?

Outside, Elsa looked at Anna. "I'm not sure any of that was exactly 'special,'" she said. "What are you going to do with all that winter gear in the middle of spring?"

Anna shrugged. "I'm sure I'll find some use for it," she said.

Olaf was looking over the supplies when a bumblebee buzzed past him. "Hello, bee," he said, and ran off after it. Olaf followed the bee, with Anna and Elsa close behind. Soon they found themselves in a field of wildflowers.

"Oh, how pretty!" Anna said. She and Elsa began to pick some flowers.

Olaf was still chasing the bee. "Where are you—Ooh!" Olaf stopped short, peering over a cliff.

"Look at this!" Olaf called to the sisters. A young reindeer was trapped on a ledge below him.

"You poor thing. How did you get down there?" Anna asked.

"Hang on," Olaf called down. "We'll save you!"

Then, turning to Anna and Elsa, he said under his breath, "How are we going to save him?"

Elsa thought for a moment. Then she waved her hands, creating an ice ramp for the reindeer to climb.

"Whoa," Olaf said, admiring the ramp.

The reindeer carefully stepped onto the ramp . . . but the ice was too slippery and he fell down!

"Now what?" Elsa asked Olaf and Anna.

"I know!" Anna said. Grabbing her bag of winter gear, she slid down the ramp. "Hey, that was fun!" she said when she landed next to the baby reindeer.

Anna quickly began to dig through her large bag of supplies. She had an important job to do!

First Anna put the snowshoes on the reindeer's hooves. Then she tied a rope around him.

"See? I told you I'd find a use for this stuff," she called up to Elsa.

Elsa grinned. "Okay, okay. You were right. Now what?"

Anna tossed the rope up to her sister. "Pull!"

Elsa and Olaf pulled with all their might. Finally, everyone was safely off the ledge.

The reindeer was so grateful to be off the side of the mountain that he gave Olaf a big kiss.

"Aww, thanks, buddy," Olaf said. Then he turned to Anna and Elsa. "Can he come home with us?" he asked.

"Of course!" Elsa said with a mischievous smile. "And I think I just might know the fastest and most fun way for all of us to get home."

Elsa grabbed Anna's and Olaf's hands and led them to the sled. "Hold on!" she cried. Then, using her magic, she created a series of snow slides. The trio zoomed down the mountain with their new reindeer friend close by.

The group slid gracefully through the castle gates and into the
ballroom.

"Whee!" Anna cried.

"Can we do that again?" Olaf asked.

Elsa smiled at her friends and then looked at the reindeer. She was
glad to be home. But she was even happier to have found a new friend.

An Icy Monster

IT WAS A BEAUTIFUL spring day in Arendelle. Queen Elsa was taking a break from her usual duties to spend time with her sister, Anna.

"Watch out!" Anna cried, speeding through the castle gates on her bike. The townspeople quickly jumped out of her way.

"That's not fair, Anna!" Elsa cried, racing after her sister. "You started before Olaf got to three!"

Behind the sisters, Olaf the snowman ran to catch up. "Wait for me!" he said. "Oooh . . . butterfly!"

Anna was almost to the finish line when a huge wall of ice appeared in front of her. She swerved to avoid it as Elsa rode past her, laughing.

"Elsa, using your powers is cheating!" Anna yelled.

"You're just jealous that I'm going to win!" Elsa called.

Just then, Elsa noticed Kristoff and Sven passing by. They looked upset. She quickly stopped her bike to see what was wrong.

Anna raced past her friends. "Ha! Winner!" she called, hopping off her bike. Then she saw Kristoff's face, and her smile disappeared. "Kristoff, are you okay?" she asked.

"We've been looking for you," Kristoff said. "Sven and I saw something huge in the forest! We tried to get a closer look, but the snow was blowing too hard. Elsa, can you control the snow so we can keep looking for it?"

"You have no idea what it was?" Elsa asked Kristoff.

"I didn't get a good look, but I think it was . . . a monster!" Kristoff said.

The sisters agreed to help and hurried back to the castle for supplies. On their way back to meet up with Kristoff and Sven, they ran into Olaf.

"Where'd you go?" the snowman asked. "I was right behind you, and then there was this butterfly, and . . ." Olaf looked at Anna's cloak. "What'd I miss?"

"We're going monster hunting!" Anna said.

"Oooh!" Olaf said. "Can I come with you guys?"

With Olaf in tow, the friends set off into the mountains to find
Sven and Kristoff's monster.

The higher they climbed, the colder it became. Before long it
began to snow . . . hard.

"Hey!" Olaf said, pointing at the snow falling on Elsa. "Now you
have a snow flurry, too!"

Olaf grabbed Elsa's hands and began to dance. Elsa laughed and
spun the little snowman around.

"Er, Elsa? A little help here?" Anna said.

Elsa turned to see her sister, Kristoff, and Sven freezing beneath a pile of snow. She quickly parted the storm to clear a path for her friends.

"Whew, that's better," Anna said, brushing herself off. "Now, if only we could find our mysterious friend that easily."

"Are we almost where you saw the monster, Kristoff?" Elsa asked a while later.

Kristoff and Sven looked at each other. "We don't remember," Kristoff admitted. "There was a lot of snow and Sven took a wrong turn."

Sven nodded.

Suddenly, a loud roar shook the mountain. Everyone froze.

"Sven you sound hungry," Olaf said.

"I don't think that was Sven's stomach, Olaf. I think it was the monster!" Anna cried.

The group started toward the noise. They hadn't gone far when they heard another roar coming from the opposite direction!

"Are there two of them?" Anna asked, stopping short.

Elsa listened. "I think the roar is echoing off the rocks!" she said.

"So how do we find the monster?" Kristoff asked.

Elsa had an idea. She stomped on the snow, and an icy staircase began to grow into the sky. Now they would be able to see the whole forest!

Anna, Elsa, and Kristoff began to climb the stairs. Below them, Sven whined. The steps were too slippery for him. He and Olaf stayed on the ground.

As Anna, Elsa, and Kristoff reached the top of the stairs, there was another great roar. "Look! The trees moved over there!" Anna said, pointing. "That must be where the monster is."

Just then, the staircase shook. Beneath them, Sven ran behind the nearest tree. But Olaf had gotten distracted.

"Hello!" he said to a bird.

"Olaf, look out!" Anna cried.

But it was too late. The mysterious monster crashed through the trees and stopped right in front of the unsuspecting snowman!

Olaf looked up. "It's Marshmallow!" he cried.

"Oh, right. Marshmallow! The giant ice monster who tried to attack us!" Kristoff said. "Shouldn't we be running far away right about now?"

Olaf gave Marshmallow a hug. "Marshmallow isn't scary! He's my friend!" Olaf smiled up at the big snowman.

"He's right, Kristoff," Anna said as she started down the stairs. "Marshmallow doesn't look very scary anymore."

Marshmallow sank to the ground and hugged Olaf closer.

"Wow, you're a really great hugger," Olaf said. "I think I'm being crushed, but only a little."

Anna looked at Sven and Kristoff. Then she looked over at Elsa.

"I think Marshmallow might be lonely," Anna said.

Marshmallow nodded.

"I'm sorry, Marshmallow," Elsa said. "I thought you would be happy in the mountains. I wish there was something we could do."

"Me too," Anna added.

Kristoff and Sven looked at each other. They had an idea. Marshmallow could help them with their ice deliveries!

A few days later, Anna and Elsa spotted a giant figure near the harbor. It was Marshmallow with Kristoff and Sven!

"Hi, Marshmallow," Anna called. "How's it going?"

Elsa smiled. "I'd say Marshmallow is much happier than the last time we saw him!"

Marshmallow nodded as he rubbed Sven's and Kristoff's heads. He was glad to be part of the team!

DISNEY FROZEN

ANNA IN CHARGE

IT WAS A BEAUTIFUL morning in Arendelle, and everyone was in a good mood. Everyone, that is, except Princess Anna.

"I wish you didn't have to go to the lichen farmers' convention, Elsa," Anna said sadly.

Elsa smiled at her sister. "I won't be gone long, Anna, I promise."

Anna sighed. She knew Elsa would be back the next day, but Anna didn't like to be away from her sister for even a little while.

"Remember, while I'm gone, you're in charge," Elsa said.

"What if I don't know what to do?" Anna asked.

Elsa gave her sister a hug. "Don't worry," she said. "I've written down some tips on how to rule. You'll be fine. And I'll be back before you know it."

In her room, Anna flopped down in her most comfortable chair. She hoped Elsa's note would prepare her for the day ahead.

Just then, there was a knock on the door, and one of the castle guards entered the room.

"Excuse me, Your Highness," the guard said. "You are needed in the throne room."

Anna's heart pounded loudly. There couldn't be a problem already. She hadn't even had time to read Elsa's note!

"Two farmers are having a disagreement," the guard explained. "They are asking for your advice on how to settle it."

Anna followed the guard to the throne room, where the two farmers were shouting at each other. Their voices were so loud that they didn't hear Anna enter the room.

"Excuse me," she said softly. But the two men kept yelling loudly.

Anna tried again, but still the farmers didn't hear her.

Finally, the guard whistled sharply. The farmers became silent and turned toward Anna.

"Thank you," Anna said to the guard. "Now what seems to be the problem, gentlemen?"

"His chickens are eating all of my corn," one farmer shouted.

"Well, his cows keep eating all the grass in my field," the other farmer yelled back.

Anna listened to the farmers. Each of them thought he was right. How was she supposed to solve their problem? Then she remembered Elsa's note.

Anna opened the note and quickly read the first few lines.

Problems can be hard to solve, Elsa had written. *You have a good heart. Do what you think is right.*

Anna bit her lip. *What do I think is right?* she asked herself silently.

Anna had listened to both sides of the argument. And she had seen that both men had a point. She thought long and hard about what advice to offer. What did her heart tell her was the right thing to do?

Finally, Anna jumped up. "I have an idea," she said. "Let the chickens eat the corn. The cows can eat the grass. And you both can share the milk and eggs!"

Anna held her breath and waited.

The farmers looked at each other. Then they slowly nodded. They both liked that idea!

As the two men walked away arm in arm, Anna smiled. She had solved her first problem of the day!

The farmers had barely left the throne room when Olina came in. "Pardon me, Your Highness," she said. "The Royal Regatta is about to start, and the Arendelle team is one person short. They might not be able to compete!"

Anna looked out the window at the boats lined up for the race.

Quickly, Anna opened Elsa's note and read the next line. *I hope you aren't bored. Don't be afraid to mix it up!*

How can I mix it up? Anna wondered. She thought hard for a minute. Then she had another idea. *I've got it! I'll help the team!*

Racing down to the water, Anna found Arendelle's team. She jumped into the boat and began to row. When the race was over, Arendelle's boat had come in second place!

Anna was happy that she had helped the team! But her day was just getting started. Next she had a visit with a group of children.

Taking a deep breath, Anna walked into the schoolroom. Once again, she pulled out Elsa's note. *You have a great big heart,* Elsa had written. *Use it to have fun.*

Anna thought of all the times she and Elsa had played together when they were children. She smiled as she remembered sliding down frozen hills and building snowmen.

Anna realized that she needed to have fun now like she'd had fun *then!*

"Who wants to play hide-and-seek?" Anna shouted. Tying a piece of cloth over her eyes, she began to count. "One, two, three . . ."

The rest of Anna's day flew by. She met with the cook to review the menu for the ice harvester dinner the following week. Then she went to see the royal papersmith to make sure the invitations to the annual spring ball were on schedule. She even inspected the troops to make sure their uniforms were spotless.

As the day wound down, Anna went back to the harbor to watch the rest of the boat races and cheer on the other teams.

When the races were finished, she went to the awards ceremony to greet all of Arendelle's guests!

Before Anna realized it, the sun was setting. Plopping down in a chair, Anna let out a huge sigh of relief. *I wonder if this is how Elsa feels at the end of every day,* she thought.

Suddenly, Anna realized that she hadn't finished reading Elsa's note. She opened the scroll. *After a busy day, it is nice to see the stars. The best view is from the roof.*

With the note in her hand, Anna climbed up to the roof. To her surprise, there was a picnic dinner laid out. Next to the food was another note addressed to her.

Excited, Anna began to read. *Good job today,* Elsa wrote. *You can be me anytime!*

Anna gasped. She didn't know if she was ready for that!

Looking back down at the note, Anna read the last few lines: *But don't worry. I'll be back tomorrow.*

Anna let out another sigh of relief. Being in charge was a lot of fun, but having Elsa home would be even better!

FROZEN

WHAT DO YOU GET A REINDEER WHO HAS EVERYTHING?

IT WAS A BEAUTIFUL day in Arendelle. Olaf danced through the meadow outside the palace gates, stopping only to smell and pick flowers. Elsa, Kristoff, and Anna trailed behind him, enjoying the sunshine and chattering happily among themselves.

Elsewhere in the meadow, Sven pranced back and forth, chasing butterflies. All in all, it was the perfect day to be outside!

Suddenly, Anna stopped walking. She turned to Kristoff, Elsa, and Olaf. "I can't wait to give Sven his birthday present—antler polish," she said excitedly. "What did you guys get him?"

"I got him a new harness," Elsa replied. "And a carrot cake!"

"I bought him some imported lichens," Kristoff said.

"It's Sven's birthday?" Olaf asked. "But I didn't get him anything."

"Don't worry, Olaf," Kristoff said. "It's actually tomorrow. Or maybe it's next week?" He shrugged. "Anyway, we always celebrated around this time of year with the trolls. They weren't big on exact dates!"

"Well, *we're* celebrating tomorrow," Anna said.

Later, at the castle, Olaf tried to think of a good birthday present for Sven. His friends had gotten Sven great gifts. Olaf wanted to give his reindeer friend something special, too.

He looked around the castle. "Ooh, a book!" he said. "Or a vase. Or a quill and some ink!"

Everything Olaf saw seemed perfect. How was he going to choose just one gift?

Olaf was looking at a large pile of gifts when Elsa appeared.

"Is everything okay, Olaf?" she asked.

"I don't know what to get Sven for his birthday," Olaf explained.

Elsa thought for a minute. "Well," she said, "sometimes the best gift is something that means a lot to you."

Olaf beamed at Elsa. She was so smart. No wonder she was queen! That was the best idea he'd heard all day.

Olaf went outside to think. As he stepped outside, his snow flurry appeared. Suddenly, Olaf knew *exactly* what to get Sven!

First Olaf needed a box. He dug through the castle closets until he found one that was just the right size.

Next Olaf went to the stables. He carefully packed the box full of the freshest hay. He wanted to make sure his gift for Sven had plenty of padding!

Finally, everything was ready. Olaf held out his hand and caught one of the snowflakes from his flurry.

"Hello, snowflake," Olaf said. "Sven is going to love you, just like I do."

Olaf was sure Sven would appreciate the cold snowflake on such a hot day. He carefully placed the snowflake on top of the bed of hay. Then he closed the box and tied a ribbon around it.

"Nice and snug!" he said. "See you soon, little snowflake!"

The next day was Sven's party. Kristoff hung balloons and streamers while Anna set up the party games.

Soon the friends were bobbing for carrots and playing pin the tail on the reindeer.

"Who wants cake?" Elsa asked, revealing a homemade carrot cake, complete with candles shaped like carrots and frosting that looked like snow!

The friends sang "Happy Birthday" to Sven, and he blew out the candles.

Olaf had been waiting all day to give Sven his gift. Finally, he couldn't wait any longer.

"Time for presents, Sven!" he said, eagerly grabbing his box for the reindeer. Everyone agreed.

Sven was delighted by the new harness from Elsa. He was thrilled with his antler polish from Anna. And he loved the imported lichens from Kristoff. Finally, Olaf handed Sven his gift.

Sven pulled the ribbon off the box, nudged the lid aside, and . . .

The snowflake was gone! Olaf looked around, confused. He didn't understand what could have happened to it.

"Wow, Olaf!" Kristoff said. "You found Sven the best gift of all."

"Huh?" Olaf said, looking at the reindeer. Sven was nose-deep in the box, munching happily.

"Aw, look at how happy he is!" Anna said.

"Olaf, how did you know that Sven's favorite treat is the first hay of the season?" Kristoff asked.

Olaf smiled. "Elsa helped me think about what Sven would like."

The snowman looked at Sven. The reindeer might not have gotten the gift Olaf *meant* to give him, but Olaf was glad he liked it all the same. He had made his friend happy, and that was good enough for him!

FROZEN FEVER
MELTING HEARTS

IT WAS A BEAUTIFUL spring day. The sun was shining over Arendelle as Anna bounced around the kitchen. She had planned a picnic for her friends and couldn't wait to get started.

"Are you ready?" Elsa asked, peeking into the kitchen.

"Almost. Most of the bags are in the hall, but can you grab that brown one?"

"What's in here?" Elsa asked.

"Just a few picnic essentials," Anna replied.

"You sure you have everything you need?" Kristoff joked.

"Maybe you want to bring the stove or perhaps . . . the whole castle?"

"I just want everything to be perfect," Anna said.

"Don't worry, Anna. It'll be great," Elsa said, "because we will all be together."

Anna smiled as she struggled with the bags. "I know, I know, but it doesn't hurt to be prepared."

"Sven and I can help you out with those," Kristoff said, taking them from her.

"Hi, everybody!" Olaf shouted as he ran toward his friends. "Oooh. Is that a real picnic basket? I love picnics. I'm so excited—let's go, let's go, let's go!"

"Let the picnic officially begin," Anna said, leading the way toward the mountains.

As they walked, Anna took a deep breath. "Those spring flowers make the air smell so sweet."

"They really do," said Elsa.

"Mmmmm!" Olaf said as he sniffed a patch of flowers. Olaf had never seen flowers that looked like those before.

He bent down closer and picked a flower.

"Hey, look!" Olaf plucked a petal from the flower and showed it to his friends. "It looks like a heart."

"Wow," Anna said. "I've never seen a flower that shape before. How pretty!"

As they continued up the mountain, something caught Anna's eye. She scooped up a leaf and showed it off. "I found a heart, too!"

"Nice," Elsa remarked. Then she began searching.

"Found one!" Elsa called. She held up a smooth heart-shaped stone.

"I bet I can find one, too," Kristoff said.

"Not before I find another," Anna replied with a grin.

Kristoff found a curved twig and bent it into the shape of a heart. "Got one!" he said happily. Then the twig snapped in half.

As the friends walked on, they continued to search for hearts. Some things looked like broken hearts. Others looked like perfect hearts. And a few didn't look much like hearts at all.

When they finally arrived at their picnic spot, Kristoff and Anna worked together to surprise everyone.

"Glad I packed those shears," Anna said with a smile.

"Wouldn't be a picnic without them," Kristoff joked.

Setting the shears aside, Anna took out the blanket. "This is the best picnic ever!" Olaf shouted as he helped spread it out.

"Oh, no!" Anna cried as she dug through the picnic basket. She had forgotten to pack the food!

Elsa couldn't believe it. "You packed candlesticks but no food?"

Anna slowly nodded.

Everyone burst out laughing—including Anna.

"Oh . . . but I did remember dessert," Anna said, happily pulling out a small box and opening it.

"Uh-oh." Anna's smile faded. Her dessert was a melted mess. "They *were* special chocolates."

Just then, it started to rain. "Oh, come on!" Anna shouted at the sky.

"What a wonderfully refreshing picnic shower!" Olaf said brightly.

The rain came down harder. "Quick! Under the blanket!" Anna said.

The group huddled together, trying to stay dry under the soggy blanket.

"Olaf, it's not supposed to be refreshing when it rains on picnics," Anna said sadly.

"But maybe it should be." Olaf smiled. "The rain is keeping us close. It's like a big cuddly hug!"

Drip. Drip. Drip. The rain started to leak through the blanket and onto their heads.

Anna groaned. This was not the perfect picnic she had pictured. "I'm sorry, everybody," she said sadly. "Should we just forget the picnic and head back to the castle?"

"The picnic's not over," Elsa said. She waved her hands and an ice gazebo appeared.

"Beautiful!" Olaf said.

"And practical," Kristoff added.

"Thanks, Elsa." Anna hugged her sister. "Maybe we can eat the melted chocolate. . . . I'm sure I brought spoons."

Elsa thought for a moment. Then, with a wave of her hands, she magically created an ice mold. "Put the chocolate into this."

It worked! Soon the friends had delicious heart-shaped frozen chocolate treats!

Anna and her friends sat together, eating their treats and watching the rain.

Everyone agreed with Olaf: it was the best picnic ever!

FROZEN FEVER
LITTLE BROTHERS

OLAF WAS ON HIS way up the North Mountain to see the snowgies Elsa had created. "I am so excited to see the little snowmen," he said to himself as he made his way up the stairs to the ice palace. "I'm going to hug little Sludge and then little Slush. . . ."

Olaf looked around. Marshmallow was sitting on the stairs as dozens of snowgies played around him.

"Isn't it exciting to have little brothers?" Olaf said.

Marshmallow sighed. He looked tired.

Olaf turned toward one of the snowgies who was running by. "Here's a nice warm hug for you—*oof!*" The snowgie bounced right off Olaf and into Marshmallow.

"Aw, these little guys are so cute!" Olaf giggled.

Marshmallow gently lifted the snowgie off his shoulder and sighed again as he put him down.

"I know you love playing with our little brothers," Olaf told Marshmallow, "but would it be okay if I took a turn?"

Olaf didn't wait for an answer. With another giggle, he faced the snowgies. "Come on, guys, let's play!" he said.

As Olaf tried to gather some of the snowgies into a group, he slipped and landed on his back. "Whoa! The floor's all slippery. Slippery? Hey, that means we can skate! I just love skating!"

Olaf got to his feet and twirled around. "Follow me, little brothers!" he shouted excitedly.

Olaf tried to encourage the snowgies to skate. He glided along the ice with ease. But the way the little snowmen spun and crashed into things made Olaf think they wanted to play another game, like tag.

"That's great! Good job, little guys!" Olaf cheered. "Attaboy, Flurry!"

Marshmallow shook his head and went outside.

"Huh," Olaf said, scratching his head. "I guess Marshmallow doesn't feel like playing right now."

Olaf looked back at the snowgies. They had tripped over one another and were now piled in a mound at the side of the room.

"You guys are so cute," Olaf said with a smile. "You're playing king of the mountain. And you're the winner, little Powder!"

As the snowgies broke free of the pile, Olaf tried to hug each of them. But they all ran away.

"Oh," Olaf said. "So you want to keep playing? That's fine. Just stay inside so nobody gets lost."

But the snowgies were already headed out the door.

"Well, outside is good, too. And Marshmallow is out there. Maybe he wants to play now," Olaf said, following the snowgies out the door.

Marshmallow seemed to be playing a new game that Olaf had never seen. He was sticking icicles into the ground, building a pen around the snowgies.

"This is great, Marshmallow!" Olaf picked up two icicles. "Now how does this game work?"

Just then, one of the snowgies bumped into Olaf, and he fell forward onto the two icicles.

"Whoa! This is fuuuun!" Olaf shouted as he zipped down the mountain on the ice. "C'mon, little brothers! C'mon, Marshmallow! Follow *meeee*. . . ."

But once again, the snowgies did not follow Olaf. Neither did Marshmallow. Instead, he turned and headed back up the stairs to the ice palace. One by one, the snowgies followed Marshmallow.

Falling into several neat lines, they trailed into the palace.

"Hey! What's everybody doing?" Olaf asked. He had never seen the snowgies looking quite so orderly and well behaved.

When Marshmallow reached the top of the stairs, he stopped and turned around. Bending down, he picked up the first little snowman in line and placed him on top of the banister. Then he gave him a firm push. The snowgie slid down, down, down!

"Hey, that looks fun," Olaf said, scurrying to the top of the stairs to help Marshmallow.

One by one—and then two by two—the snowgies took their
banister rides. "This is a great idea, Marshmallow," Olaf said.

No matter how quickly the giant snowman sent the snowgies
down the banister, the line didn't seem to get any shorter. The little
snowmen raced up the stairs, eager to slide down again and again.

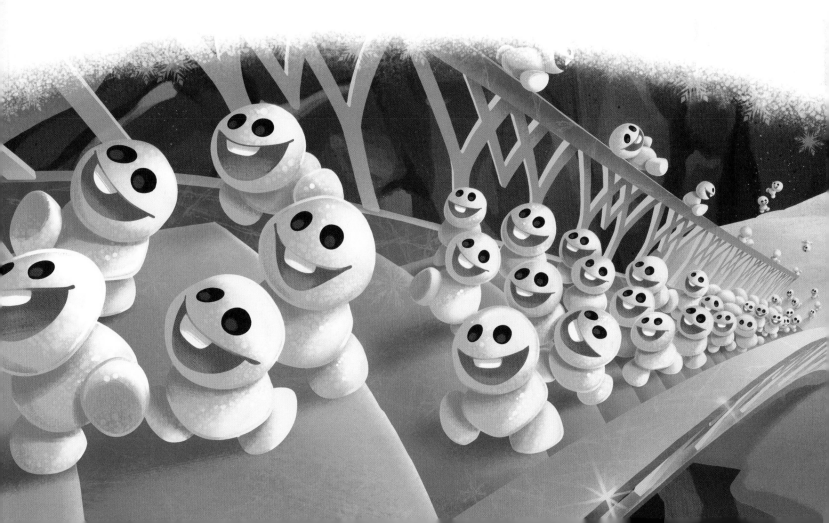

The sliding continued until it was almost dark outside, when the snowgies finally seemed to tire themselves out.

Yawning and dragging their feet, they shuffled back inside the ice palace. One by one, they piled up on top of each other and drifted off to sleep. It had been quite a busy day for the little snowmen!

Before long, every snowman was snoring, even Marshmallow, who now had a smile on his face. He'd had a fun day!